WATERSHIP™ DOWN

Hazel the Brave

Diane Redmond

RED FOX

A Red Fox Book

Published by Random House Children's Books
20 Vauxhall Bridge Road, London SW1V 2SA

A division of The Random House Group Ltd
London Melbourne Sydney Auckland
Johannesburg and agencies throughout the world

www.watershipdown.net

Illustrations by County Studio, Leicester

1 3 5 7 9 10 8 6 4 2

Printed and bound in Italy by Lego SPA

THE RANDOM HOUSE GROUP Limited Reg. No. 954009

www.randomhouse.co.uk

ISBN 0 09 940345 5

This story represents scenes from the television series, Watership Down,
which is inspired by Richard Adams' novel of the same name.

The rabbits were inspecting their new burrows on Watership Down.

'Isn't this the biggest warren you've ever seen?' said Blackberry proudly.

'It's too big for just us,' said Hazel. 'We need more rabbits to join us.'

'But where do we find new rabbits?' asked Bigwig.

'Efrafa,' said Hazel. 'I've sent Kehaar there to have a look round.'

Efrafa was a dark warren that had been dug deep under the roots of a fallen tree.

Kehaar swooped down and landed on a ledge nearby. He saw General Woundwort standing on a high platform and two frightened rabbits standing in front of him.

Woundwort spoke to the guard.

'What is their crime, Vervain?' he asked.

'They tried to escape,' said Vervain.

'Escape?' Woundwort's eyes flashed in anger. 'All rabbits know they can never leave Efrafa. Take them to the dungeons!'

Kehaar flew back to Watership Down and told Hazel what he'd seen. 'Efrafa no good. Woundwort fierce leader. He punish rabbits if try run away!'

'So there *are* rabbits who would join us,' said Hazel.

'Plenty, but many guards keep watch,' said Kehaar.

'Then we must go to Efrafa and help them escape,' said Hazel. 'I'll take Bigwig and Fiver with me.'

Bigwig and Fiver looked shocked. They didn't like the sound of Efrafa or its leader. But Hazel had made up his mind. They would leave the next day.

At Efrafa, they hid behind some brambles and watched a group of rabbits eating. Kehaar pointed to two of them. 'Those Primrose and Blackavar – they try run away.'

When the rabbits were close enough to hear him, Hazel whispered, 'I've come to help you escape.'

Then Vervain came over. Hazel ducked out of sight, but Fiver stepped on a dry twig, which snapped loudly.

'Who's there?' called Vervain.

Before the guard could find out, Primrose and Blackavar bolted into the woods.

Vervain chased after them and brought them back to the warren.

'Come on, let's go!' said Bigwig.

Hazel shook his head. 'Primrose just saved my life. I'm not leaving without her.'

Suddenly Fiver's whole body began to shake. 'The only way out is to go straight through. If two go in, then out come two.'

'He's having a vision,' said Hazel. 'Two of us must go into Efrafa to get Primrose and Blackavar out.' He turned to Fiver. 'Will you come with me, little brother?'

They stepped out of the brambles and walked up to one of the guards.

'Take me to your leader!' said Hazel.

The astonished guard looked at him, then he led them down a maze of dark tunnels to the dungeon.

As the opening closed, a figure crept out of the shadows.

'Primrose!' cried Hazel.

'So they caught you, anyway,' she sighed.

'Actually, no!' said Hazel. 'We want to be here. We've come to speak to the General.'

'Is he mad?' asked Primrose.

'No,' said Fiver. 'Just very brave.'

Then Vervain appeared. 'The General will see you now,' he said.

The guard took the rabbits to the gathering place at the entrance of the warren.

Woundwort climbed onto his platform. He looked down at Hazel. 'What do you want, Outsider?' he growled.

Hazel came forwards. 'I have two questions to ask,' he said.

Woundwort nodded and Hazel continued. 'Do you prefer peace or war?'

'War!' said the General.

'Do you prefer life or death?'

'Death!' roared the General. 'I have answered your questions. Now you will be punished for your foolishness. Guards, seize them!'

Two guards charged forwards, but just as they were about to strike, Fiver began to tremble. 'Stormhaven is destroyed!' he wailed.

Woundwort looked shocked. 'What are you saying? Stormhaven was my home.'

'I can see a weasel,' moaned Fiver. 'It's coming towards a doe – her name is Laurel.'

'Laurel was my mother!' said Woundwort.

'Laurel pushes young Woundwort away from danger. She faces the weasel. And dies.'

Fiver collapsed on the ground, as his vision ended.

Woundwort was very moved by what he'd heard. He came down from his platform and slowly hopped outside. 'Who is that rabbit?' he asked Hazel. 'How does he know my story?'

'He's a wise rabbit from a great warren,' Hazel answered loudly. 'We have soldiers all around.'

Behind the brambles, Bigwig understood Hazel's message. 'He wants us to pretend to be an army of rabbits,' he told Kehaar. 'Come on. Shake the bushes.'

When the guards saw the brambles moving, they dashed forwards to attack.

'Stop!' Hazel called out. 'You've seen what my brother can do. Harm any of us and your leader will suffer more.'

The guards turned to look at their General, who just stared at the ground. They didn't know what to do.

'Let the prisoners go,' said Vervain.

Fiver turned and fled, but Hazel stopped to whisper to Primrose, 'Wait for me, I'll come back for you.' Then he disappeared through the brambles.

The rabbits raced out of Efrafa with Kehaar flying high above them. Suddenly the gull let out a screech. 'Run! Run! Woundwort follow.'

The General had recovered from his shock and was angry that Hazel and Fiver had escaped. 'Find them!' he roared.

Woundwort and his guards searched the countryside, but they couldn't find Hazel and his friends.

'I'll get you, Outsider!' Woundwort raged. 'I'll find your warren and destroy your people!'

In the woods below Watership Down Hazel, Bigwig and Fiver heard his voice echo through the treetops. They crouched undercover and waited until everything was quiet. Then, when they were sure the General had gone, they scampered up the hill to home.

'We were lucky to escape,' said Bigwig, as they lay curled up safe and warm with their friends on Watership Down.

Fiver nodded. 'We made an enemy today,' he whispered. 'But you were brave, Hazel.'

'Woundwort doesn't frighten me!' said his big brother. 'I'm going back to Efrafa and soon.'